Taking Care of Tekno Pup
The Official Guide to Tricks and Training

TAKING CARE OF TEKNO
THE ROBOTIC PUPPY

The Official Guide to Tricks and Training

TRACEY WEST

SCHOLASTIC INC.

New York Toronto London Auckland Sydney
Mexico City New Delhi Hong Kong

ISBN 0-439-29504-1

12 11 10 9 8 7 6 5 4 3 2 1   1 2 3 4 5 6/0

Printed in the U.S.A.
First Scholastic printing, January 2001

Contents

Taking Care of Tekno Pup
The Official Guide to Tricks and Training

Congratulations!

You are the proud owner of Tekno the Robotic Puppy. Lucky you! Soon you will be playing with your puppy, teaching it tricks, and learning all about its personality.

This book will help you get the most out of your relationship with Tekno. On these pages you'll find clear instructions for training Tekno, solutions to problems, and ideas for fun things you can do with your puppy. There is even a special diary section in the back where you can keep track of the things you and Tekno do together.

As you read the book, keep your eye out for Tekno Tips. These juicy bites of information will help you become a premium puppy owner.

By now, Tekno is anxious to come out of its box and play. So turn the page and get ready to enter the wonderful, woofy world of Tekno!

Chapter One

So You've Always Wanted a Puppy

What kid doesn't dream of having a puppy? They're cute, they're fun, and they can become great friends. But let's face it, puppies can be a real handful to take care of. That's what makes Tekno the Robotic Puppy so terrific. It's like having a pet, without all the fuss and mess.

Here are just some of the reasons why taking care of Tekno is easier than taking care of a real puppy:

• Real puppies need to be housebroken. But you'll never have to put down newspaper for Tekno. And when it's cold, or rainy, or snowy, you never have to take Tekno for a walk outside.

• Oh no! Your real puppy chewed up your favorite pair of sneakers. But Tekno will never take a bite out of your stuff — or out of you, for that matter.

• Fleas love to live on real puppies. But those itchy insects steer clear of Tekno's robot body.

• *Achoo!* Real puppies make some people sneeze. But no one's ever been allergic to a robot.

• Buying dog food every week can empty your pocket pretty fast. But Tekno the Robotic Puppy is satisfied to eat its bone over and over again.

• Visits to the vet are important to keep a real puppy healthy. But you never need to bring Tekno to the vet — unless you want to show it off, of course.

Isn't Tekno great? But don't worry — just because Tekno is easier to take care of than a real puppy doesn't mean that it's not as much fun as a live dog. Tekno can do lots of things that real puppies do:

• Tekno can move and sound just like a real puppy. It eats, sleeps, walks, barks, whines, cries, sniffs, begs, wags its tail, wiggles its ears, and more!

• Tekno can learn tricks and respond to your commands.

• Tekno can keep you company all day long.

Pounce on over to the next chapter to find out more about Tekno!

TEKNO TIP

Some people have both kinds of puppies — a Tekno robotic puppy, and a real puppy. Real dogs are very curious about Tekno. Sometimes they even try to play with Tekno! And Tekno responds to the noise and movement of real dogs. This can be fun, but be careful. Keep an eye on Tekno when it is with a real dog to make sure neither puppy gets hurt.

Chapter Two

Meet Tekno

Your Tekno is more than a toy. Tekno is a robot with a powerful computer brain. Tekno's brain has been programmed to act like an eight-week-old puppy.

What's the big deal about a computer brain? Well, that means that Tekno can do some thinking on its own, just like a real puppy. Tekno will decide if it wants to obey your command. Sometimes it will, and sometimes it won't. If Tekno is hungry or lonely, its computer brain tells it to whine so you know to feed it and play with it. When it starts to get dark, Tekno gets sleepy. And Tekno's brain also lets it know when someone is knocking on your door.

Each Tekno may look alike, but they can behave differently in small ways. Your Tekno may wag its tail when you scratch behind its ears, while your friend's Tekno may bark or wiggle its ears instead. That's one of the fun things about Tekno — getting to know its personality. The more you play with Tekno, the more you will learn about how to make it happy. Tekno has not been programmed to do anything bad, but it will whine, whimper or growl if it is unhappy.

In chapter four you will learn how to recognize all of Tekno's moods. But first, it's time to take your Tekno out of the box!

TEKNO TIP

To find out more about the scientists who created Tekno, go to www.tekno-robot.com. Click on Top Secret FBI Files. Type in username "Tekno" and password "4K9INFO." Make sure you enter the capital and lowercase letters exactly as they are here.

Chapter Three

First Things First

By now you are probably itching to take Tekno out of its box — and it's not because you have fleas! You're anxious to see all the cool things Tekno can do. Believe it or not, taking Tekno out of its case is probably the most difficult thing you'll ever have to do with Tekno. You will need an adult to help you.

When you open the top of the box, you will find a screwdriver and a blue manual. These are very important! Read page three of the owner's manual. That will tell you how to get Tekno out of the box.

Once an adult has helped you remove Tekno, you must do the following things:

1. Remove the paper package from Tekno and untie any plastic straps you find.

2. Make sure you remove Tekno's silver bone and the piece of card with the card trick on it.

3. Pull the tab from Tekno's side. This will start Tekno's programming.

4. Look for a clear shield on each of Tekno's ears. Remove the shields.

You've probably noticed the on/off switch on Tekno's belly. If you can, resist the urge to turn Tekno on right away. Remember that blue manual? Take a few minutes and read it through. It's short, and easy to understand. Go ahead and take a look at it now. Then come back to this page.

Did you read the manual? Great! You're ready to turn on Tekno. Turn on the switch, put Tekno on the floor, and get ready to be amazed! Tekno will start to bark and walk right away. If possible, put Tekno in a room with lots of open space. This will give Tekno plenty of room to explore.

Now it's time to find out what Tekno can really do.

TEKNO TIP

Your Tekno was not programmed to be a boy or girl. That is up to you. You may wait to see what kind of personality your puppy has before you decide. Learning about your puppy's personality may help you give it a name, too.

Chapter Four

The Basics

A Tekno that's just been turned on is a bundle of energy. It barks, yips, walks, bumps into things, and whines. You may think Tekno is too much puppy for one owner to handle, but don't worry. There are some simple things you can do to control Tekno's behavior.

What's All This About Sensors?

Your owner's manual talks a lot about Tekno's sensors. So what is a sensor, anyway? It's pretty simple. A sensor is something that can sense a change in the environment. For example, a sensor might detect if the lights go off, or a loud noise.

There are four important sensors to locate before you can start training Tekno.

1. **HEAD SENSOR:** This is the round button on top of Tekno's head.

2. **NECK SENSOR:** This is the rectangle on the back of Tekno's head.

3. **NOSE SENSOR**: Tekno's black nose is a button you can push.

4. **MOUTH SENSOR**: That tiny line below Tekno's nose can also be pushed like a button.

Find each one of Tekno's sensors and press it. You'll see that pressing each one changes Tekno's behavior.

Making Tekno Happy

You can press Tekno's sensors to teach it how to do tricks. We'll get to that later. First, you can use the sensors in simple ways to make an unhappy Tekno happy again.

How can you tell what kind of mood Tekno is in? It's not too difficult. A happy Tekno will do one or more of these things: wag its tail, wiggle its ears, flash its eyes, pant, or bark. An unhappy Tekno will cry, whine, beg, moan, or even growl. An unhappy Tekno's ears may stay down.

It's easy to make Tekno a happy puppy once more. You can do it using the four sensors we just talked about:

• Pat Tekno on the head. Press Tekno's **HEAD**

sensor and it will think it is being patted on the head. Tekno loves this.

• Scratch Tekno behind the ears. Press Tekno's **NECK** sensor and it will think it is being scratched behind the ears.

• Feed Tekno. Being hungry makes Tekno unhappy. Feed Tekno by pressing its bone against its **MOUTH** sensor. Make sure you press hard enough. Tekno will make munching noises when it is eating. Like any puppy, Tekno will eat almost anything. Just press the treat against Tekno's mouth sensor and let it chomp away. The manual recommends feeding Tekno once a day, but you can feed Tekno as often as you like — robot dogs can't become chubby puppies!

• Talk to Tekno. Tekno loves to be around humans, and hearing voices lets Tekno know it is not alone. Tekno especially likes it when you call its name.

• Make noise. Clap your hands, stamp your feet, sing a song — all of these things make Tekno happy.

Playing With Tekno

Now you know how to make Tekno happy. Well, Tekno can make you, happy, too. Here are some cute things Tekno can do:

• Tekno can lick your face. That's right! Tekno might not have a tongue, but it you put its face against your cheek, it will make a licking sound. This only works if both the **NOSE** sensor and **MOUTH** sensor are pressed against your cheek.

• Tekno can sniff. If you press an object against Tekno's **NOSE** sensor, Tekno will take a whiff. (And because Tekno's a robot, it can even smell your dirty socks without fainting!)

• Tekno can beg. Wave Tekno's bone in front of its eyes. Tekno may walk toward you, whine, or even beg for the bone. Of course, it makes Tekno very happy if you reward him with a treat after it begs for one!

• Tekno can stop walking on command. Just press Tekno's **NOSE** sensor once. Tekno will stop and make a little bark. The stop doesn't last long, though, so get ready for Tekno to start moving again.

When Playtime Is Over

You can leave Tekno on all day, just like a real puppy. But just like a real puppy, Tekno needs almost constant attention. Tekno may sit quietly for awhile, but as soon as it hears a noise or senses a movement it will want to play again. Since you cannot play with Tekno every minute of the day (even though you might want to!) you can choose to turn Tekno off when you are not playing with it.

Many Tekno owners find that this is the easiest way to take care of Tekno. They turn Tekno off to keep their puppy from getting bored or lonely. You may decide to do this, too. The only bad thing about this is that if you have taught Tekno any tricks it will forget them once it is turned off. You will have to teach Tekno its tricks all over again. Programming most tricks is easy, but if you programmed Tekno's alarm clock, you might not want to go through all those steps again.

Of course, no puppy is active twenty-four hours a day — not even Tekno. Some owners find that Tekno's sleep function gives them all the relief they need from their playful puppy!

Time to Sleep

Tekno goes to sleep at night, when it is dark and quiet. That's thanks to another set of sensors, Tekno's **LIGHT** sensors. Tekno's light sensors are in its eyes. They tell Tekno's computer brain when it gets dark. When that happens, Tekno makes a little noise, like a whimper. Then you will notice that Tekno's eyes change. Its normally round eyes become slits. Finally, Tekno's eyes will shut off, and it will start to snore. That means Tekno is asleep.

As long as Tekno is in a dark, quiet, room, it will continue to sleep. It will stay still and quiet most of the time, although some puppy owners report that Tekno sometimes snores during the night.

To wake up Tekno, you can make a loud noise, turn on the lights, or touch it. Tekno can also wake up on its own if you set its alarm (see chapter six: Advanced Tricks).

Putting Tekno to sleep is another way to keep Tekno quiet if you are not able to play with it. You don't have to wait until it's nighttime — simply put Tekno somewhere dark and quiet. You might want to make a Tekno Dog House (chapter nine) for this purpose. That way you don't have to turn off Tekno and lose its programming.

TEKNO TIP

Tekno can only walk in one direction. It cannot turn around. If Tekno walks into a wall or another object, it will make a grinding noise. Don't panic — this will not hurt Tekno in any way. Soon Tekno will stop walking. When it stops, pick up Tekno and get it walking in another direction. (If you pick up Tekno when it is walking, you might get a finger caught in its leg.)

TEKNO TIP

If you own two Tekno robotic puppies, they may keep each other from falling asleep. While one dog is starting to snore, the other dog may bark and wake it up. To stop this from happening, you may want to let your pups sleep in separate rooms.

Chapter Five

Tekno's Tricks

You're probably having a lot of fun with Tekno by now. But guess what? You're only just beginning. There's even more Tekno can do.

Tekno can do eight everyday tricks. But to teach Tekno a trick, you need to program its computer brain. You do that by pressing Tekno's sensors in different combinations.

Now that you're ready to teach Tekno tricks, it's time to learn about a new button — the **MODE** button. This button is on Tekno's left shoulder.

If you've found the **MODE** button, you can teach Tekno tricks. It isn't as hard as you might think. There are three things you can do to make sure you master each trick on the first try.

1. Read through the instructions first before you try to teach Tekno a trick.

2. Work with a partner. Have your partner read aloud the instructions while you program Tekno.

3. Program each step one at a time, SLOWLY! Take your time. If you miss a step, or do it wrong, the trick will not work.

Ready to teach Tekno a trick? Here's how to do it. First, you need to program Tekno. Then you need to ask Tekno to perform the trick. It's all about pressing the sensors and the **MODE** button.

Teach Tekno to Speak

What to do:
1. Press Tekno's **HEAD** sensor.
2. Hold for three seconds until you hear a beep.

How to get Tekno to perform the trick on command:
Yell Tekno's name or clap your hands.

What will happen:
Tekno will bark, wag its tail, or move its ears in happiness.

How to stop the trick:
Pat Tekno on the head or give it a treat.

Teach Tekno to Fetch

What to do:
1. Press Tekno's **NECK** sensor.
2. Hold for three seconds until you hear a beep.

How to get Tekno to perform the trick on command:
Yell Tekno's name or clap your hands.

What will happen:
Tekno will walk.

How to stop the trick:
Pat Tekno on the head or give it a treat.

Teach Tekno to Howl at the Moon

What to do:
1. Press the **MODE** button and the **HEAD** sensor at the same time.
2. Hold for three seconds until you hear four beeps.
3. Press the **HEAD** sensor one more time.

How to get Tekno to perform the trick on command:
Cover Tekno's eyes or place it in a dark room.

17

What will happen:
Tekno will make a howling noise.

How to stop the trick:
Press the **MODE** button and the **HEAD** sensor at the same time. Hold for three seconds until you hear four beeps. Then press the **MOUTH** sensor once.

Teach Tekno to Say Words in English

What to do:
1. Press Tekno's **MODE** button and **NOSE** sensor at the same time.
2. Hold for three seconds until you hear four beeps and then, "Thanks!"
3. Press the **NOSE** sensor one more time.

How to get Tekno to perform the trick on command:
Wave your hand in front of Tekno's eyes, feed him, or just play with him normally.

What will happen:
Tekno will say "TEKNO" when you press its **MODE** button or when it gets light or dark. It will say "THANKS" if you feed it. It will sometimes say "COOL!" when it is happy or when you play with it.

How to stop the trick:
Press the **HEAD** sensor and **MODE** button at the same time. Hold for three seconds until you hear four beeps. Press the **HEAD** sensor one more time.

Teach Tekno to Laugh

What to do:
1. Press the **MODE** button and the **NOSE** sensor at the same time.
2. Hold for three seconds until you hear four beeps and then, "Thanks!"
3. Press the **HEAD** sensor to hear Tekno laugh.
4. Press the **NOSE** sensor one more time.

How to get Tekno to perform the trick on command:
Talk to Tekno or make a loud noise.

What will happen:
Tekno will laugh and say "Squooze Me" or "Sorry."

How to stop the trick:
Press the **MODE** button and **HEAD** sensor at the same time. Hold down for three seconds until you hear four beeps. Press the **HEAD** button one more time.

Teach Tekno to Sing and Dance

What to do:
1. Press the **MODE** button, the **NOSE** sensor, and the **MOUTH** sensor at the same time.
2. Hold for three seconds until you hear four beeps.
3. Press and release the **MODE** button. You will hear a beep.

How to get Tekno to perform the trick on command:
Press the **HEAD** sensor. You will hear one beep. Then hit **MODE**. Tekno will perform his first song-and-dance routine. Tekno knows three routines altogether. To hear the other two, wait until the routine is over. Start from the beginning. When you press the **HEAD** sensor to start the trick, wait until you hear two beeps, and press the **MODE** button again. To hear the third song, wait until you hear three beeps, and then press the **MODE** button.

What will happen:
Tekno will do sing one of three songs: 1. "Happy Birthday" 2. "The William Tell Overture" 3. A Chopin tune. While it sings, it will wag its tail, wiggle its ears, and move its legs in a joyous puppy dance.

How to stop the trick:
Wait for the routine to end or press the **RESET** button on Tekno's belly.

Teach Tekno to Make Rude Noises

What to do:
1. Press the **MODE** button and the **HEAD** sensor at the same time.
2. Hold for three seconds until you hear four beeps and then, "Thanks!"
3. Press the **NOSE** sensor one time and hear the "rude noise" sound.

How to get Tekno to perform the trick on command:
Tekno will do this on its own for about ten minutes.

What will happen:
Tekno may not make a mess like a real puppy, but it can still get gas! It will make a rude noise and say "Squooze Me" or "Sorry."

How to stop the trick:
Press the **MODE** button and **HEAD** sensor at the same time. Hold down for three seconds until you hear four beeps. Press the **HEAD** button one more time.

Teach Tekno to Sing a Wake-Up Song

What to do:
1. Press the **MODE** button and the **NECK** sensor at the same time.
2. Hold for three seconds until you hear three beeps.
3. Press the **HEAD** sensor and listen to the first song.
4. If you like that one, press the **MODE** button. If not, press the **HEAD** sensor again to hear another song. Press **MODE** to choose that song instead. You can also wait until you hear a third choice.

How to get Tekno to perform the trick on command:
Tekno will perform the song automatically when it wakes up after being asleep.

What will happen:
Tekno will sing one of the three songs from his song-and-dance routine.

How to stop the trick:
Press the **MODE** button and **HEAD** sensor at the same time. Hold down for three seconds until you hear four beeps. Press the **MOUTH** button one more time.

You can keep track of the tricks you teach Tekno in your puppy diary in chapter ten, and in the special chart in chapter eleven.

TEKNO TIP

Tekno can only learn one trick at a time. For example, if you teach it to talk, it will keep talking. But if you reprogram it to laugh, it will laugh instead. If you want it to talk again, you will have to reprogram it. You will also have to reprogram a trick if you turn Tekno off, if you hit the reset button, or if its batteries run out. For this reason, make sure you DON'T LOSE THE MANUAL or this book. They will come in handy if you want to do tricks with Tekno again and again.

Chapter Six

Advanced Tricks

If you've practiced the tricks in chapter five, you've got the hang of programming your robotic puppy. That's good, because Tekno knows two advanced tricks that take some tricky programming. If you can teach Tekno these tricks, you'll be a master puppy trainer!

Don't worry if the instructions look hard. Just remember the three rules from chapter five: Read the instructions first, work with a partner, and perform each step SLOWLY. If you do that, you'll get these tricks right on the first try.

Setting Tekno's Alarm Clock

You can teach Tekno to wake up exactly when you want it to in the morning. Tekno will either sing or make a fire alarm noise — it's up to you. Here's what you do:

1. Press the **MODE** button for three seconds until you hear a beep.

2. Tekno's eyes will be round. That means Tekno is ready to tell time in the A.M. mode. Those are the hours from midnight to noon.

3. Find out what time it is. Let's say it is 8:10 P.M. Your first job is to let Tekno know the hour — 8 P.M. Remember, Tekno is in the A.M. mode. To get to P.M., hit the **HEAD** sensor twelve times.

4. Now Tekno's eyes should be slits. That means Tekno is in P.M. mode. Now you need to hit the **HEAD** sensor eight times — one for each hour.

5. Double check to make sure you have programmed the right time. Hit the **MODE** button and you'll hear a beep for each hour. If you hear eight beeps, and you'll know that Tekno now knows it is 8 P.M. Tekno's eyes will return to normal. If you hear the wrong number of beeps, you have to hit the reset button and start over.

6. Now you need to tell Tekno the minutes. Look at the current time and divide the minutes into five-minute segments. Each segment equals one beep. So five minutes is one beep, 10 minutes is two beeps, 15 minutes is three beeps, etc.

7. Press the **HEAD** sensor for each five-minute segment. In our example, it is 8:10 P.M., so that

means pressing the sensor two times. Press the **MODE** button when you are done. Tekno's eyes will flash. You will also hear the number of beeps you entered.

8. If the number of beeps is incorrect, press the **MODE** button and **NOSE** sensor at the same time and hold for three seconds. If the number of beeps is correct, simply press the **MODE** button once more. When Tekno's eyes stop flashing, it means you've done it. Congratulations! Tekno knows what time it is.

9. Now you can set Tekno's alarm. Press the **MODE** button and **MOUTH** sensor at the same time for three seconds. When you hear a beep, it means you are in alarm mode.

10. Select a wake-up time. Then repeat steps 3–7 to set the wake-up time. (Remember, if you want to wake up in the morning — A.M. time — you don't need to go into P.M. mode.)

11. Tekno will automatically wake you up by barking and wagging its tail. If you would prefer to wake up to a fire alarm sound, you need to act right after you set the wake-up time. Press the **MODE** button and NOSE sensor for three seconds until you hear a beep.

Tekno's alarm will shut off by itself. To end the alarm function, hit the reset button. And remember — if you turn Tekno off or if its batteries die, you will need to reprogram the clock and the alarm.

Tekno's Card Trick

Real puppies can do lots of amazing tricks, but they are definitely not able to perform magic card tricks. That's where Tekno's got them beat. Tekno can actually tell you the number on a playing card you are pointing to. This tricks takes some practice, but once you master it, you're friends and family will be begging to see it again.

Practice doing the trick on your own a couple of times. When you're ready to show it off, use this script to help you polish your act. First, place Tekno on a flat surface, like a tabletop. Then put the card labeled "Tekno's Card Trick" on the table in front of Tekno. IMPORTANT: Make sure the card is flat on the table, and that the arrows are pointing toward Tekno's eyes. If the card is not in the right position, this trick will not work!

Then, it's time to begin your peformance. Address your audience in your best show-business voice:

Ladies and gentlemen, boys and girls, allow me to introduce you to Tekno, a technological wonder. This robotic puppy can walk, talk, sing, and dance. But that's not all! This pup will perplex you by performing a magnicifent magic card trick. That's right — Tekno will tell you what card you are pointing to. Do I have a volunteer from the audience?

Get a friend or family member to stand in front of Tekno. Ask your volunteer to put a finger on one of the playing cards.

Prepare to be amazed! I will now program Tekno with its secret robot commands.

Program Tekno. Press the **MODE** button and **NOSE** sensor for three seconds. Hold until you hear four beeps and Tekno says, "Thanks!" Press the **MOUTH** sensor and Tekno will play a tune. While the tune plays, tell your volunteer what he or she is supposed to do.

Next I will press Tekno's nose. When I do that, Tekno will ask you to move your finger. He will do that by barking or howling. One of Tekno's eyes will light up. As soon as Tekno barks or howls, please move your finger in the direction of Tekno's eye. If Tekno asks you to move in a direction and there is no card to move to, leave your finger right there. Think you can handle that? Then let's get started!

Press Tekno's **NOSE** sensor once. You will hear a beep. When your volunteer is ready, hit the **HEAD** sensor once. Tekno will start giving commands rather quickly. Make sure your volunteer moves a finger each time Tekno barks or howls. When Tekno is ready, it will bark the number on the card that your volunteer is pointing to: four times for the four of hearts, three times for the three of clubs, etc. Then Tekno will laugh. If you followed the rules correctly, Tekno will always give the correct answer.

Thank you! Thank you! Do I have another volunteer?

To get Tekno to perform the trick again, simply hit the **HEAD** sensor. as many times as you like. When you're done, hit the **MODE** button and Tekno will be ready to do something else.

So, did you teach Tekno its advanced tricks? If so, don't forget to enter them into the chart in chapter eleven. Once you've taught Tekno all the tricks, you'll be a Top-Rate Tekno Trainer!

TEKNO TIP

Tekno's advanced tricks can be a challenge —
especially setting the alarm clock. See if an
adult can help you learn these tricks. And don't
feel bad if you don't master them right away.
Everyone needs practice!

Chapter Seven

Start a Puppy Play Group

Tekno loves being around other robotic puppies. If you know other people who own a Tekno, see if you can get together and play with your puppies. Your Tekno will have fun, and you'll probably learn something new about your Tekno, too. Here's some things you can do if you form a Puppy Play Group:

Let the Puppies Play Together

Tekno knows the barks and sounds of other robotic puppies. When it hears them, it will bark, wag its tail, walk — all of the things it does when it is happy.

When two Teknos meet, give them a chance to size each other up. Put the dogs down on the floor, facing each other, and watch what happens. Your puppies may walk toward each other and sniff each other, just like real dogs do! Then they may bark and start to walk around. That is how they play. Watch your puppy's behavior and make a note of it in the diary in chapter ten.

Puppy Obedience School

Working with a partner is a great way to learn how to teach your dog tricks. Take turns teaching your dogs the tricks in chapter five. First one of you can read the instructions aloud while the other programs the dog. Then switch.

You can also compare your puppies to see how they learn and perform tricks. Your dog may pick up tricks quickly, while your friend's dog is more stubborn. Or your dog may have trouble learning to say certain words, while your friend's dog has no trouble at all. Keep notes in your diary about what things your dog is good at, and what tricks it needs to work on.

Have a Puppy Race

This works best if you have four people and two dogs. Have your helpers hold your puppies in place. You and your friend should sit on the floor across from your dogs — about five feet away. On the count of three, the helpers should press each dog's **NECK** sensor for three seconds. After the beep, start calling your dog to you. The puppy to reach its owner first is the winner.

More Puppy Games

Find out how well you communicate with your puppy by playing these simple games. Use a stopwatch if you have one.

• See who can get their puppy to go to sleep the fastest.

• See who can make their puppy bark the most times in two minutes.

• See who can make their puppy wag its tail the most times in sixty seconds.

• See who can get their puppy to perform the most tricks without using the owner's manual.

TEKNO TIP

Sometimes Tekno puppies look a little different from each other — their eyes might be different colors, for example. But for the most part, it is hard to tell your puppy apart from someone else's. To make sure your puppy doesn't get mixed up with your friend's, try marking it in some way. Tie a ribbon around one of its legs, or write its name on a piece of masking tape and stick it somewhere on its body.

Chapter Eight

More Fun With Tekno

So your Tekno has learned all its tricks. It gets along well with other puppies. So you think that's all there is? Not a chance! The amount of fun you can have with Tekno is only limited by your imagination.

Here are some cool things you can do with, and for, your Tekno. If you come up with more ideas, why not write them in your diary in chapter ten?

Dance With Tekno

Program your Tekno to do one of its dance routines. Then get down on all fours. See if you can copy Tekno's moves. If Tekno shakes its leg, shake a leg. If Tekno steps forward, step forward. If Tekno wags it tail . . . you get the idea. Get your friends together for a Tekno Dance Party. It's Puppy Night Fever!

Hold a Dog Show

Invite your friends and family to come meet your Tekno. When your audience is seated, explain what Tekno is and what it can do. Demonstrate how Tekno can do simple things, like sit and beg. Then show off some of your favorite tricks. If you've mastered it, finish the show with Tekno's Magic Card Trick.

You can hold a dog show with your friends, too. Assign each one of Tekno's abilities or tricks to a different person. One friend can demonstrate how Tekno begs. Another person can show how Tekno laughs, etc. Give everyone a chance to participate.

When your dog show is over, give each dog a blue ribbon made from construction paper to show that each Tekno is a number one pup!

Make a Tekno House

Many real dogs have a special place to rest and sleep. Your Tekno can have one, too. You'll need:

- an adult to help you
- scissors
- an empty cardboard box, at least 12" high
- silver paint or aluminum foil
- Tekno's bone
- pencil
- construction paper
- glue

Get an adult to cut off the top flaps of the box. Turn the box upside down. Have your adult helper cut out a doorway on one side, large enough for Tekno to fit through. Paint the box silver, or cover it with aluminum foil. Then trace Tekno's bone several times onto construction paper. Cut out the bones and glue them to the house when the paint is dry.

That's it! It's all ready for Tekno to move in. This house will come in handy if you want to give Tekno a quiet place to sleep. You can even put Tekno in his house during the day and let him take a nap when you're pooped from playing with your puppy pal.

Puppy Puzzle

See if you can find the Tekno words hidden in this puzzle. Look for words up, down, across, backward, and diagonally.

Words to find

bark	dog	lick	robotic	Tekno
beg	eat	pet	sing	trick
dance	fetch	puppy	sniff	wag
	laugh		tail	

```
D   G   O   N   K   E   T   D
P   L   I   C   K   T   S   A
E   S   I   N   G   A   N   N
A   R   O   B   O   T   I   C
T   E   H   C   T   E   F   E
T   K   X   G   Y   P   F   Q
A   R   G   P   U   P   P   Y
C   A   O   E   T   A   I   L
W   B   D   T   B   S   L   R
```

37

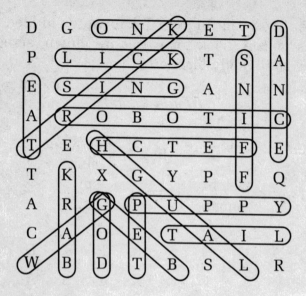

TEKNO TIP

Talk to your friends who have Tekno robotic puppies. What fun things do they do with their dogs? It's a great way to get ideas.

Chapter Nine

Solving Problems

Having trouble with your Tekno? Most problems are easy to solve. Here are some of the most common problems people encounter with their puppies.

My Tekno just whines and wimpers all day. What's wrong?
You might not be spending enough time with Tekno. Try playing with Tekno — pat its head, scratch behind its ears, and call out its name. Tekno might be hungry, so you could try feeding it a bone. If those things don't work, Tekno might want you to teach it a trick. But don't forget — all Teknos are different. Some are whinier than others. The best thing to do is to keep playing with your Tekno until you learn what makes it happiest.

I taught Tekno a command or a trick, but it didn't do it!
First, make sure you did the trick correctly. Try doing it again, slowly. Get someone you know to help you to make sure you are doing it right. If

you did everything right, don't worry. Tekno is temperamental, just like a real puppy. Sometimes it will obey you, and sometimes it won't. Just keep practicing. That's what being a puppy owner is all about!

I keep calling Tekno, but it doesn't bark or walk or anything. It just sits there.
Keep trying. Speak louder or move closer. Clap your hands. Tekno will usually respond when it hears a noise.

Tekno is on, but it won't respond to ANY of my commands. It won't move or bark.
Don't worry. Tekno isn't dead! It just needs new batteries. Tekno uses four AA alkaline batteries. You shouldn't try to change the batteries yourself — get a parent to help you. Battery-changing instructions are on page sixteen of the manual.

When I turn Tekno on, its eyes flash off. Then I hear a long, beeping sound.
This also means that your battery is dead. Follow the same steps as above.

I was playing pretty rough with Tekno, and its legs fell off!
Tekno may be a robot, but it's not indestructible.

The good news is that if one of its legs falls off, it's pretty easy to pop it back into place. The same goes for Tekno's ears, too. But please do not try this unless Tekno has a real problem!

I'm trying to program Tekno do to a trick, but its eyes just keep flashing. It won't beep the way it's supposed to.
You are probably in clock mode by mistake. Press the **MOUTH** sensor or hit the reset button.

TEKNO TIP
The best way to keep your Tekno problem-free is to take good care of it. Don't let Tekno fall or crash. It's okay to bring Tekno outside, but keep it away from dirt or water. While it might be fun to give a real puppy a bath, giving a robotic puppy a bath is bad news!

Chapter Ten

"Tekno and You":
Your Robotic Pet Diary

You and Tekno are sure to have lots of special times together. Now you won't forget any of them. Use the pages of this weekly diary to keep track of your puppy's learning and to record special memories.

This diary belongs to:

_ _

My robotic puppy's name is:

_ _

I got Tekno on this date:

_ _

My Tekno

What do you like best about your robotic puppy?

What three words describe your puppy best?

What makes your robotic puppy a good pet?

What is your favorite trick?

What does your puppy do that makes you laugh?

My Tekno Tips

I discovered these tips on my own
for taking care of Tekno:

1. _____

_____

_____

2. _____

_____

_____

3. _____

_____

_____

4. _____

_____

5. _____

_____

_____

My Tekno Activities

I made up these activities on my own
for playing with Tekno:

1. _____

_____

_____

2. _____

_____

_____

3. _____

_____

_____

4. _____

_____

5. _____

_____

_____

Week of _

My puppy learned how to _ _ _ _ _ _ _ _ _ _ _ _ _
_ _
_ _
date_ _

My puppy did the funniest thing!_ _ _ _ _ _ _ _ _
_ _

My puppy played with _ _ _ _ _ _ _ _ _ _ _ _ _ _ _
date_ _

I took my puppy to_ _ _ _ _ _ _ _ _ _ _ _ _ _ _ _ _
date_ _

My puppy is great at_ _ _ _ _ _ _ _ _ _ _ _ _ _ _ _
_ _

My puppy and I need to work on_ _ _ _ _ _ _ _ _
_ _

Week of _

My puppy learned how to _ _ _ _ _ _ _ _ _ _ _ _ _
_ _
_ _
date_ _

My puppy did the funniest thing!_ _ _ _ _ _ _ _ _
_ _

My puppy played with _ _ _ _ _ _ _ _ _ _ _ _ _ _ _
date_ _

I took my puppy to_ _ _ _ _ _ _ _ _ _ _ _ _ _ _ _ _
date_ _

My puppy is great at_ _ _ _ _ _ _ _ _ _ _ _ _ _ _ _
_ _

My puppy and I need to work on_ _ _ _ _ _ _ _ _
_ _

Week of _

My puppy learned how to _ _ _ _ _ _ _ _ _ _ _ _ _ _
_ _
_ _
date_ _

My puppy did the funniest thing!_ _ _ _ _ _ _ _ _
_ _

My puppy played with _ _ _ _ _ _ _ _ _ _ _ _ _ _ _
date_ _

I took my puppy to_ _ _ _ _ _ _ _ _ _ _ _ _ _ _ _ _
date_ _

My puppy is great at_ _ _ _ _ _ _ _ _ _ _ _ _ _ _ _
_ _

My puppy and I need to work on_ _ _ _ _ _ _ _ _
_ _

Week of _

My puppy learned how to _ _ _ _ _ _ _ _ _ _ _ _ _
_ _
_ _
date_ _

My puppy did the funniest thing!_ _ _ _ _ _ _ _ _
_ _

My puppy played with _ _ _ _ _ _ _ _ _ _ _ _ _ _ _
date_ _

I took my puppy to_ _ _ _ _ _ _ _ _ _ _ _ _ _ _ _ _
date_ _

My puppy is great at_ _ _ _ _ _ _ _ _ _ _ _ _ _ _ _
_ _

My puppy and I need to work on_ _ _ _ _ _ _ _ _
_ _

49

Chapter Eleven

Trainer Checklist and Obedience Certificate

A puppy gets rewarded for good behavior with treats. You have worked hard to train your puppy, so you deserve a reward, too! Keep track of the tricks you teach your puppy on the next page. When the checklist is filled out, you get a special certificate. Cut that page out of the book, fill it in, color it, and hang it on your wall so everyone will know what a perfect puppy trainer you are!

Trainer Checklist

My Puppy Mastered This Trick On:

❏ Speak _____

❏ Fetch _____

❏ Howl at the Moon _____

❏ Say Words in English _____

❏ Laugh _____

❏ Sing and Dance _____

❏ Make Rude Noises _____

❏ Sing a Wake-Up Song _____

❏ Alarm Clock _____

❏ Magic Card Trick _____

This certifies that

_____

is a

Top-Rate Tekno Trainer

of a robotic puppy.

_____

finished its training on

_____

Congratulations!